CHADRON (NE) STATE COLLEGE

W9-BLF-395

Books by Janice May Udry
published by
Albert Whitman & Company

WHAT MARY JO SHARED
ALFRED
BETSY-BACK-IN-BED
END OF THE LINE
NEXT DOOR TO LAURA LINDA
IF YOU'RE A BEAR

WHAT MARY JO WANTED

JANICE MAY UDRY ***Pictures by ELEANOR MILL***

Albert Whitman & Company, Chicago

LIBRARY OF CONGRESS CARD NUMBER 68-9123
PUBLISHED SIMULTANEOUSLY IN CANADA BY GEORGE J. MCLEOD, LTD., TORONTO

LITHOGRAPHED IN THE UNITED STATES OF AMERICA

WHAT MARY JO WANTED

Every time Mary Jo saw a dog, any dog—big or little, black, white, old or young—she wished it belonged to her.

"I would rather have a dog than anything on earth," she said at least twice a week, usually at the dinner table. She sighed. "I'd be the happiest person in this town if I had a puppy." She often read the ads in the classified section under "Pets for Sale" out loud to her parents.

"Puppies must be trained. It takes a lot of patience," said her father.

"I'd love to train a puppy!" said Mary Jo. "I'd do it all myself!"

“Puppies cry at night when you first bring them home,” said her father. “Nobody gets any sleep.”

“They cry because they’re lonesome. I’ll be the one to get up in the night and talk to my puppy,” said Mary Jo.

"They must be fed every day. They must have fresh water. They should be brushed. They must be given baths," said her father.

"I'd do it! I'd do it!" said Mary Jo. "I *want* to feed and brush and wash a dog."

"A good dog owner must take the full responsibility for her pet," said her father.

Responsibility was a word Mary Jo had heard a lot lately—ever since her sister had received a canary for her birthday. She was being responsible for her bird, but she was quite a bit older than Mary Jo. Besides, a bird in a cage was not as great a responsibility as a puppy.

"I would be responsible," said Mary Jo.

Mary Jo read dog books by the dozen. She drew pictures of dogs. She wrote dog stories and dog poems. One morning she put a two-page theme by her father's plate, "Why I Want a Dog."

It looked as if fate were on Mary Jo's side when a new pet store opened downtown.

She showed the big opening day ad in the newspaper to her parents. She read: "Special for This Opening. Small, lovable, mixed-breed puppies. Only $19 while they last!"

"I would like a badger," said Mary Jo's brother. "Do they have any badgers?" Jeff had just been looking at a picture of a badger family in a new book from the library.

"Can't we go down to see the new pet store? And the puppies?" Mary Jo begged.

"All right, Mary Jo. I believe you're old enough to take care of a puppy," said her father.

"Oh," shouted Mary Jo. "Get your coats, everybody! Let's go!"

PET

"They *are* cute," said Mary Jo's mother when they stood gazing down at a little pen full of puppies in the new pet store.

"Cute!" said Mary Jo. "They're the sweetest creatures ever born in this world!"

Her father laughed. "Which one do you want?"

Mary Jo barely hesitated. One little furry baby had wobbled over to lick her fingers the minute she knelt beside the pen.

"This one," she said. "He came right to me. He's the best, the smartest, the most lovable!"

"Have him wrapped up then," said her father.

"Wrapped up?" said Mary Jo. Then she saw that her father was joking. He got out his billfold.

The first thing the family did when they got home was to put newspapers all over the kitchen floor. Mary Jo turned her old doll bed sideways in the doorway so that the puppy could not go into the rest of the house.

"It's only until you're housebroken," she told him when he sniffed inquiringly at the doll bed. He reached playfully for her shoe string and looked up into her face.

"You cute, darling baby!" cooed Mary Jo picking him up and hugging him.

"Be sure to call the vet this week and make an appointment," said Mary Jo's father. "He should have his puppy shots right away."

Mary Jo and her friend Laurie spent hours deciding on a name for him. They made lists and poured over the section of names at the back of the dictionary.

Jeff suggested "Mr. Picklepone." That was the silliest name he could think of.

In the end they decided on "Teddy" because the puppy looked so much like a small teddy bear, and he even squeaked.

He squeaked and cried—*especially* at night. No matter how cozy Mary Jo made his bed in the kitchen or how many times Teddy yawned at bedtime, he always woke as soon as everyone was in bed and the house was still. He woke and cried as if his heart would break. Mary Jo put a night-light in the kitchen, in case he was afraid of the dark. She gave him a little snack at bedtime, in case he was hungry. She put an old toy dog in bed with him, hoping he would think it was a companion. But he didn't.

Mary Jo staggered sleepily from her warm bed out to the kitchen a dozen times a night. She talked to Teddy and sang to him. As long as she was there, he was happy. He tried to get her to play as if it were the middle of the day instead of the middle of the night, and he licked her with his loving puppy tongue. As tired as she was, Mary Jo could never feel angry with him because he was so joyful each time she appeared at the kitchen door and stepped over the doll bed.

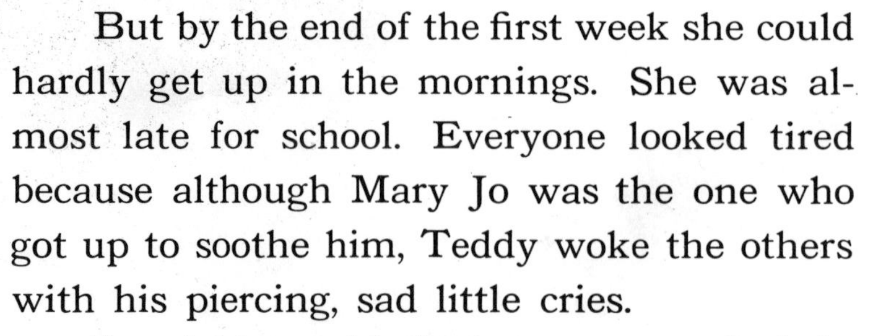

But by the end of the first week she could hardly get up in the mornings. She was almost late for school. Everyone looked tired because although Mary Jo was the one who got up to soothe him, Teddy woke the others with his piercing, sad little cries.

A neighbor told them to wrap a clock in flannel and put that beside Teddy in the bed. "He'll hear the tick and think it's another puppy," she told them. But it didn't fool Teddy for one minute.

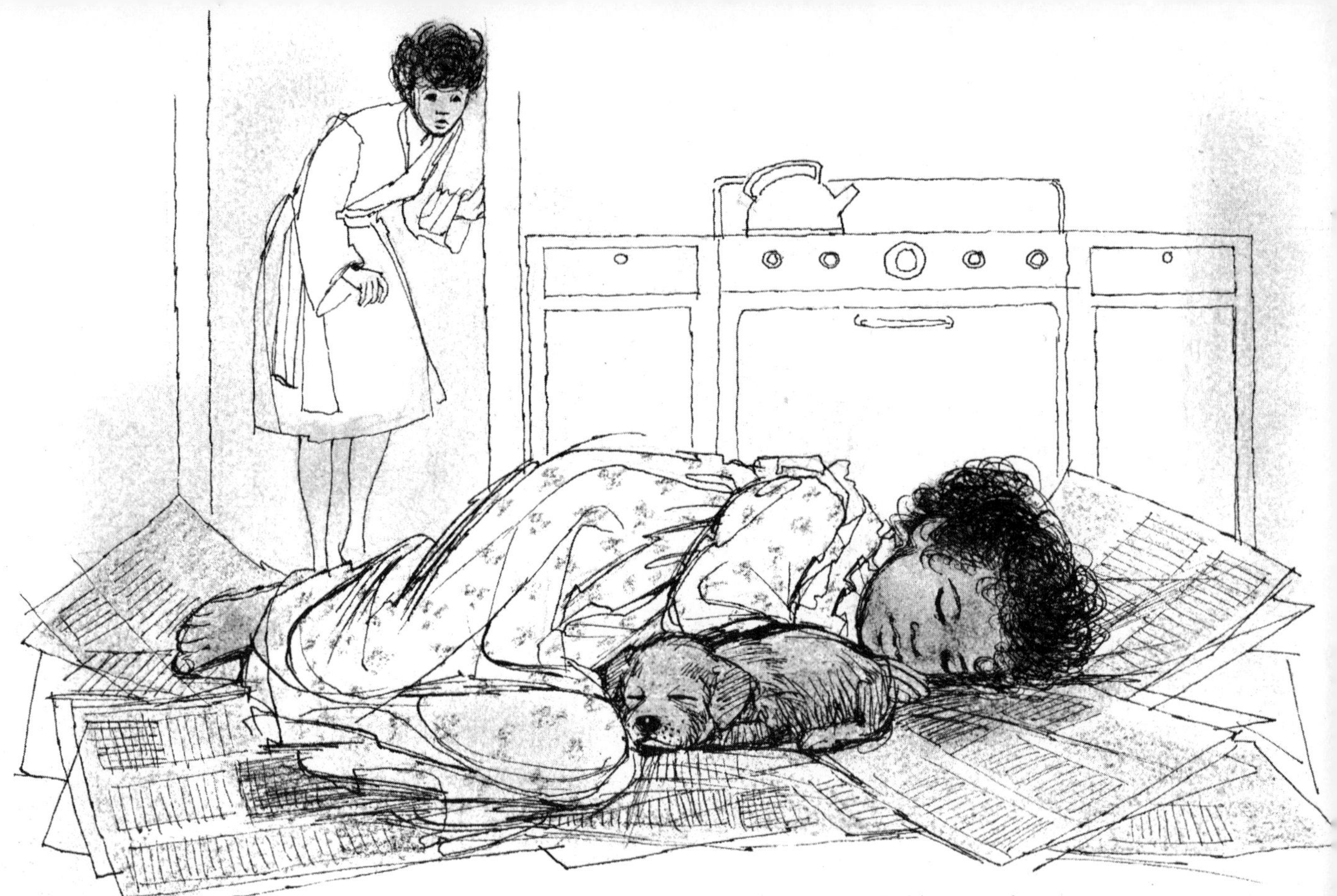

Finally one morning Mary Jo's mother found her asleep on the paper covered kitchen floor.

"Is this ever going to end?" Mary Jo's mother asked at the breakfast table. "I don't ever remember hearing of any puppy crying as many nights as this one has."

"Some of them get used to being alone faster than others I guess," said Mary Jo's father wearily. "But I'm beginning to wish we had never seen that dog!"

"I'm responsible," thought Mary Jo. "I've *got* to think of something to keep Teddy quiet."

That afternoon when she went to the basement to get some old newspapers for the kitchen floor she saw something that gave her an idea.

After dinner that night Mary Jo said, "You'll be able to sleep tonight. I've thought of a way to keep Teddy quiet."

"What is it?" asked her mother.

"You'll see," said Mary Jo. She went down to the basement.

Her parents heard her lugging something up the stairs. It was an old folding cot.

"I'm going to sleep in the kitchen until Teddy is housebroken and can sleep in my room," she said.

Her mother and father looked at each other.

"Why not?" said her father. "That's probably the only thing that will solve the problem."

And it did. Teddy slept without making one squeak all night with Mary Jo on the old cot just above his basket.

Mary Jo thought it was fun to sleep in the kitchen. It was cozy to hear the refrigerator hum and the faucet over the sink drip now and then. In the glow of the night-light she liked to see the toaster and the coffeepot gleaming. If she woke at daybreak, it was pleasant to see the new day arriving in the kitchen so early. There was a window to the east, so sunlight came to the kitchen first.

And it was fun to surprise her mother by slipping quietly around early to set the table for breakfast and then hopping back into bed and pretending to be asleep when her mother came to the kitchen.

They both pretended that it was the work of the kitchen elf.

"Mary Jo, wake up!" her mother would say. "Do you know that the kitchen elf was here again?"

"Was he really?" Mary Jo would say, sitting up. "I didn't hear a thing!"

And she hugged Teddy and tried not to giggle.

❖ *About the Author*

Sometimes stories for children are close to life in the sense that they are direct and realistic. Sometimes they are true to the child's feeling about his world even though literal realism is missing. Certainly part of Janice May Udry's success in the picture book field grows from her ability to write both kinds of stories.

In *What Mary Jo Shared* Mrs. Udry tells of a child searching for something original and all her own to share at school. On the other hand, Peter meets talking animals in *If You're a Bear,* but he discovers something that is true: what is right and appropriate for one circumstance may not be for another.

Like many authors who write for girls and boys, Mrs. Udry blends impressions from her childhood with observations of her own family. Janice Udry grew up in Jacksonville, Illinois, and graduated from Northwestern University. Books entered her life in a professional way when she assisted in the university library; little children were her concern when she taught in a Chicago nursery school.

Because her husband, Richard Udry, is a sociologist and teacher, the Udry family has made several moves from one college or university campus to another. Recently they migrated east from California to North Carolina, where they and their daughters, Leslie and Susan, live in Chapel Hill. There Mr. Udry is a public sociologist and directs a project to evaluate national family planning programs. He, too, is an author.

With well over a dozen books published, Mrs. Udry has found an individual place in the world of children's books. Her *A Tree Is Nice* was awarded the Caldecott Medal in 1957, and *The Moon Jumpers* was a runner-up for the same honor in 1960.

Mrs. Udry was especially happy when her first story about Mary Jo brought a warm response from so many children, parents, teachers, and librarians. Mary Jo, it seems, has become a very real little girl, one anybody can believe in and expect to meet some day—perhaps with her new puppy.